My Little Gol

WHALES

The editors would like to thank Paul L. Sieswerda, president and CEO of Gotham Whale, for his assistance in the preparation of this book.

BY **BONNIE BADER**

ILLUSTRATED BY **STEPH LABERIS**

 A GOLDEN BOOK • NEW YORK

Text copyright © 2024 by Bonnie Bader
Cover art and interior illustrations copyright © 2024 by Steph Laberis
All rights reserved. Published in the United States by Golden Books, an imprint of Random House Children's Books, a division of Penguin Random House LLC, 1745 Broadway, New York, NY 10019. Golden Books, A Golden Book, A Little Golden Book, the G colophon, and the distinctive gold spine are registered trademarks of Penguin Random House LLC.
rhcbooks.com
Educators and librarians, for a variety of teaching tools, visit us at RHTeachersLibrarians.com
Library of Congress Control Number: 2022949694
ISBN 978-0-593-56984-9 (trade) — ISBN 978-0-593-56985-6 (ebook)
Printed in the United States of America
10 9 8 7 6 5 4 3 2 1

blue whale

bowhead whale

sperm whale

orca

beluga

They can sing. They are smart. They are giant, yet graceful. They can dive deep and jump high. And they can live for a very long time. What are they?

Whales!

Let's dive in.

Whales might look like fish, but they are mammals, just like humans. Mammals breathe air, give birth to babies, and produce milk to feed their young.

So how can a mammal breathe underwater? It can't.

When a whale is swimming, it can hold its breath for a long, long time. When it needs air, the whale comes up to the surface and breathes through the blowhole on the top of its head. You can see its spout. It's like breathing through nostrils—if your nose was on top of your head!

Some whales, like this minke, have a dorsal fin, which can be seen rising above the water when it swims near the surface. The dorsal fin helps keep a whale steady, so it doesn't roll around in the water.

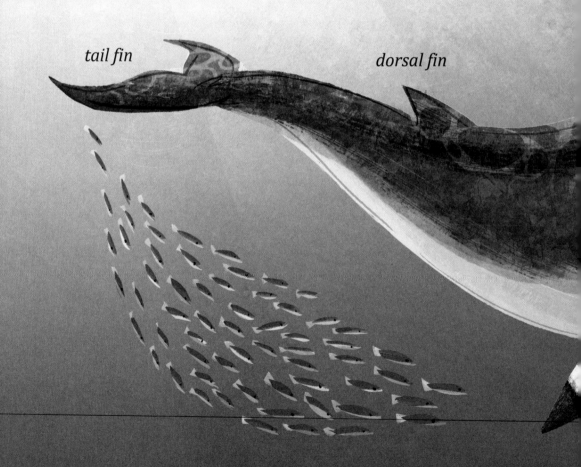

tail fin

dorsal fin

The pectoral fins, also called flippers, help the whale steer while swimming.

With their tail fins—or flukes—a whale can move forward, and fast!

pectoral fins

Layers of fat called blubber keep the whale warm when it travels in cold water.

There are two types of whales: toothed and baleen. And you can see how they're different when they open their mouths.

The whale with all the pointy teeth is—you guessed it—the toothed whale. Different types of toothed whales eat different things. Some eat fish and squid. And some eat mammals such as seals and even other whales!

Is that hair inside a baleen whale's mouth? No, that's called baleen. Baleen is made of keratin, the same material that makes up your hair and fingernails. If baleen breaks, it keeps on growing, just as hair and nails do. Baleen whales eat small fish, shrimp, and tiny sea creatures called krill. And baleen whales have two nostrils in their blowhole.

It's dinnertime, and this blue whale is hungry for some krill. She opens her mouth wide and takes a huge gulp of water—and the small sea creatures swimming in it. Then she uses her giant tongue to push the water out. The baleen acts as a filter, making sure the water goes out but the tasty krill stay in.

The blue whale is the largest animal to ever live on earth, weighing up to two hundred tons. Its tongue alone can weigh as much as an adult elephant! It can live about ninety years and grow to the length of three school buses parked end to end.

krill

Blue whales live in all the earth's oceans, except for the Arctic Ocean. These gentle giants travel alone or in groups, called pods, of one to two other blue whales. They communicate with each other by making very loud sounds.

Male humpback whales, which are also baleen whales, don't just communicate—they sing! Their underwater melodies sound like moans and cries and howls. These whale songs can be heard from miles away.

Watch out! A killer whale is approaching. Even though the female humpback is too large for him to eat, her baby is just the right size. The mama humpback protects her baby as they swim away fast.

The baby is safe. The mama humpback whale leaps high out of the water. Then she dives back in—like doing a giant cannonball—and makes a huge splash.

This is called breaching. No one knows for sure why whales breach, but scientists think it's a way for whales to communicate with each other. Whatever the reason, a breaching whale is a beautiful sight!

Another baleen whale jumps out of the water. This is a bowhead whale. It is called that because its upper jaw is shaped like a bow that's used to shoot arrows. The bowhead whale can live for a very, very long time: around two hundred years!

Bowheads have the thickest layer of blubber of any sea mammal. This is a good thing because they live in the freezing Arctic waters. *Brrr!*

Here comes a hungry sperm whale. It spots a giant squid, grabs it with its sharp teeth, and swallows the squid whole.

The sperm whale is the largest of the toothed whales, and it has the largest head of any animal. Its head is twenty feet long—that's bigger than a full-grown giraffe!

Meet the narwhal. Some people call it the unicorn of the sea. Can you guess why?

This toothed whale looks like it has a horn sticking out of its head. But it is really a tooth or a twisty tusk!

Narwhals live in the cold Arctic waters and travel in pods of as many as a hundred other narwhals. The pod spots a school of codfish. A narwhal strikes a cod with the tip of its tusk. This stuns the fish so it can't move. Quickly, the narwhal gobbles it up. What a delicious meal!

The beluga whale is related to the narwhal. And like the narwhal, it swims in the cold Arctic waters. The beluga's white coloring helps it blend into the ice to protect it from other animals that want to eat it, such as polar bears and killer whales.

The top of a beluga's head is called a melon. It's very squishy and helps to direct its sounds.

The beluga can be quite noisy. It makes lots of different clicks, chirps, buzzes, groans, and roars. The sounds allow it to communicate and hunt for food. To hunt, the beluga uses sound waves that travel through the water and bounce back (or echo) after bumping into something, like a crab. This lets the beluga know where to find its next meal.

The killer whale, or orca, also uses sound waves for hunting. This orca has located a seal.

Splash! The orca jumps out of the water to catch the seal with its teeth.

Now get ready for a whale of a fact: an orca is actually a dolphin!

There are about forty different kinds of dolphins, and orcas are the largest. All dolphins are whales, but not all whales are dolphins.

Whales swim in all the oceans of the world. Some whales are small. Some are huge. All are amazing.

minke

narwhal

humpback

What is your favorite whale?